Enid Blyton's
NAUGHTY
AMELIA JANE!

This book
was given
to Gemma
From Carly
when she
had read
It.

First published 1969
Reprinted 1993

Published by Dean, an imprint of
The Hamlyn Publishing Group Limited,
Michelin House,
81 Fulham Road,
London SW3 6RB,
England

Copyright © Darrell Waters Limited 1939

Enid Blyton is a registered trademark of Darrell Waters Limited

ISBN 0 603 03271 0

Printed in Italy

Enid Blyton's
NAUGHTY
AMELIA JANE!

DEAN

CONTENTS

CONTENTS

CHAPTER I
NAUGHTY AMELIA JANE!

THE toys in the nursery were very friendly with the small brownies who lived in the bushes below the nursery window. The brownies had no wings, but they managed to climb up the tall pear tree and get in at the window whenever it was open. So you can guess that the toys and the brownies had many a good game!

There was one very naughty toy, who often made the others really angry. This was Amelia Jane, a big, long-legged doll with an ugly face, a bright red frock, and long black curls. She hadn't come from a shop, like the others, but had been made at home. Shop-toys nearly always have good manners, and

7

know how to behave themselves—but Amelia Jane, not being a shop-toy, had no manners at all, and didn't care what she said or did!

Once she poured a jug of milk down the golliwog's neck, and that made him wet and uncomfortable for two days. Another time she threw a woollen ball up so high that it went into the goldfish globe, and made the poor goldfish jump almost out of his skin. Then, when the teddy bear climbed up to get the ball out of the water, Amelia Jane climbed up behind him, gave him a push—and there was the poor bear, spluttering away in the water, and trying his hardest to swim, whilst the goldfish darted at him in fury.

Dear dear, how Amelia Jane laughed,

and how all the other toys shouted at her! Whatever would she do next?

The next thing she did was to catch a bee in a matchbox, and then, when the sailor doll wanted to light his pipe for a smoke, she gave him the matchbox, pretending that there were matches inside. You can imagine how scared he was when a bee flew out and stung him on the nose!

"Amelia Jane, you are a perfect nuisance," said the toys angrily. "Can't you settle down and be good like us? One day you will do something that will get us all into trouble!"

"Pooh!" said Amelia Jane rudely. "I shan't!"

But she did do something very naughty indeed the next time.

She was hunting about in Nurse's work-basket for a thimble to play with, when she came across Nurse's scissors. Ho! Now she could have a fine game of cutting!

So she took the scissors and began to snip-snip-snip everything! The other toys were sitting in a corner playing a game of snap, and they didn't notice at first what Amelia Jane was doing. They wouldn't let Amelia play snap with them because she said "Snap!" when it wasn't, and took away all their cards.

So Amelia Jane had a lovely time all by herself. She snipped a hole in the curtains, and then she snipped another!

Then she went to the hearth-rug and cut a whole corner off that! Then she found Nurse's handkerchief on the floor, and do you know, she cut it into twenty-two tiny pieces! It was one of Nurse's best hankies too, with a pretty lace edge. But Amelia Jane didn't care about that!

Then she went to the carpet and began to snip little bits of it here and there. The carpet was a green one with red roses, and wherever Amelia could see a rose, she snipped! Wasn't it dreadful of her?

The toys took no notice. They were having such a lovely game. Amelia grew cross with them for being happy without her. So what do you suppose she did? She went up behind the pink rabbit

and snipped his tail off!

Goodness! You should have seen how he jumped!

"Oooooooh!" he yelled. "She's snipped my tail off! Look! Oh, the wicked, wicked doll!"

"And look what else she's done!" cried the toys in horror, pointing to the spoilt hanky, the snipped rug, and the cut carpet. "And look, she's spoilt the curtains too. Oh, what trouble we shall get into! Nurse will know it must be the toys, and she will throw us all into the dustbin! Oh!"

The toys stared in horror at all that the naughty doll had done. The pink rabbit cried bitterly, for he felt dreadful without a tail. Oh dear! How he would be laughed at, now that he hadn't a tail! The golliwog put his arm round him and comforted him.

"Don't worry, Bunny," he said. "We shall all love you just the same, even if you don't wear a tail, and look rather like a guinea-pig!"

The pink rabbit cried all the more loudly when he heard that. "I don't want to be like a guinea-pig!" he wept. "I want to be like a rabbit! I hate Amelia Jane! Punish her, Golly! She is a very wicked doll!"

Amelia Jane laughed. She loved doing naughty things. She liked seeing all the toys staring in horror at the mischief she had done. Ha, ha! That would teach them to play "Snap" without her!

"Give me those scissors," said the golliwog sternly.

"Shan't!" said Amelia Jane, twirling them round in her big hand.

"I said, 'Give me those scissors!'" ordered the golliwog, his black hair standing all on end with anger.

"I said 'Shan't!'" said Amelia Jane, "and if you talk to me like that, Golly,

I'll cut all your hair off! Then you'll look like a black Chinaman!"

"You naughty, wicked doll!" said the golly, in a fury. But he didn't dare to try to take the scissors away, for they had very sharp points, and he really was afraid that Amelia Jane would cut his lovely black hair off. He was very proud of it, and he didn't want to lose any.

"Whatever shall we do?" said the teddy bear. The toys all looked at one another in despair.

Then they heard a little scraping noise at the window, and they saw their friends, the brownies, creeping in at the crack at the bottom.

"Hallo, Toys! You look very miserable!" said the brownies,

scrambling down from the window-seat to the floor. "What's the matter? Have you lost a shilling and found a penny?"

"No," said the toys. "Just look here, brownies, at what Amelia Jane has done!"

"I say!" said the brownies, staring at all the damage. "Why did you let her have scissors? And look, she still has them. You ought to take them away from her before she does any more mischief."

"She won't let us have them," said the golly. "She says she will cut all my black hair off if I try to take them from her."

"Oho, we'll soon see to that!" said the biggest brownie at once. "Scissors, come to me!"

He waved his little gold wand—and immediately the scissors flew out of Amelia Jane's hand and went to the brownie. He caught them and gave them to the golliwog.

"Oh, thank you," said the toys gratefully. "I suppose you couldn't help us to mend all these dreadful holes and slits that Amelia has made?"

"Oh yes, I think so," said the biggest brownie. "We'll just go and get our needles and thread, and come back to help you. We'll sew everything so that you won't see even a tiny stitch! We are very clever at stitching, you know. Once we sewed all the petals on a daisy that had lost hers in a rainstorm— and you really couldn't see that they were not growing! As for that handker-chief, we'll use a bit of magic for that, and all the bits will join together so that the nurse will never know it has been cut!"

The brownies fetched their needles and thread, and soon they were sitting on the carpet and on the rug, mending all the slits and cuts, and two of them

mended the curtains. Then the biggest
brownie put a spell into his needle and
sewed on the bunny's tail again. It
didn't hurt a bit because of the spell.
The bunny was so grateful.

The handkerchief was mended too—
and everything was put right.

"There!" said the brownies, in

delight. "We've done all we can!"

"We can't thank you enough!" said the toys. "You may be sure that if ever we can help you in return we will!"

"As for Amelia Jane," said the biggest brownie, "I should keep her a prisoner in the toy cupboard until she says she is sorry and won't be naughty any more. Here is a spell that will keep her there!"

The golly took the spell. It was in a little box, and when it was taken out and blown over Amelia, she had to stay where she was put. The toys surrounded the naughty doll, pushed her into the cupboard, and then blew the spell at her. She couldn't move her legs! There she had to stay!

At first she was very angry. Then she was frightened, and begged to be set free. She saw the toys going happily about their play, and she wanted to join them. It was dreadfully dull in the toy cupboard all alone except for a box of bricks that never said a word.

"I'm sorry, Toys! Do set me free!" begged Amelia Jane. "I will try very hard not to be naughty any more."

"If we could be sure you would do good things and not naughty ones, *we would* set you free," said the golly. "But we don't trust you. You have never done a good or brave thing all the time you have been with us."

Amelia Jane was just going to answer him when there came a tapping at the window. The toys looked up. A small red robin was there. He looked most excited.

"What is it?" shouted the toys, swarming up to the window-seat.

"It's the brownies!" said the robin. "They have been attacked by the goblins! They have hidden in the old hollow tree, but the goblins are cutting it down! Can you rescue them?"

"How?" said the golly, upset and bothered to hear such bad news.

"I don't know," said the robin. "You'll have to think of something— but hurry, because at any moment the goblins may get them!"

He flew off, and the toys crowded together, all talking at once.

"Toys, Toys, I have a plan!" cried Amelia Jane from the cupboard. "Let me fly the toy aeroplane out of the window. It will frighten the goblins terribly, and they are sure to run away. Then, before they come back, the brownies can get into the aeroplane and I'll fly it safely back here!"

"All right!" shouted the toys, excited. "It's a good idea. Set her free, Golly."

So Amelia Jane was set free. The aeroplane was run up to her, and she got in. Rr-rr-rr-rr-rr! It shot up into the air and out of the window. How exciting it was! Amelia was a bit afraid of falling out, but she managed to guide the aeroplane to the hollow tree. Then down she flew—and all the little goblins who were cutting down the tree to get at the brownies inside, cried out in horror:

"Run! Run! The aeroplane is coming down on top of us!"

They scattered in fright. Amelia stopped the aeroplane and landed by the hollow tree. She called to the brownies:

"Brownies! Quickly! Get into my aeroplane! I've come to rescue you!"

The brownies all shot out of the hollow tree at once and clambered into the plane. When the goblins saw what was happening they gave a shout of rage and ran to the aeroplane at once—but it was too late. Rr-rr-rr-rr-rr! It rose into the air, and flew straight back to the nursery window. In two minutes the brownies were safe in the nursery with the toys, and *how* pleased they were!

"Amelia Jane has turned over a new leaf," said the brownies, in surprise. "Brave Amelia Jane! Thank you so much for rescuing us!"

"Don't mention it!" said Amelia. "I am trying very hard to be good now."

And you will be pleased to hear that she certainly *was* good for a little while, but I'm afraid it didn't last for very long!

CHAPTER II
AMELIA JANE GETS A SHOCK

WELL, for a little while Amelia Jane was very good—and then, oh dear, she forgot all her promises, and became really naughty! The things she did!

She took a needle and cotton out of Nurse's work-basket, and sewed up the sleeves of the teddy bear's new coat when he wasn't looking. So when he went to put on his coat, he simply could *not* put his arms through the sleeves anyhow! He just couldn't find the way in—because the sleeves were sewn up! How Amelia Jane laughed to see him!

The next night she hid behind the curtain and began to mew like a cat.

The toys were not very fond of Tibs the cat, because he sometimes chewed them. So they all stopped playing and looked round to see where Tibs was.

"I can hear him mewing!" said the teddy bear. "He must be behind the door."

But he wasn't. Amelia mewed again.

The toys hunted all about for the cat. They even looked in the coal-scuttle, and under the hearth-rug, which made Amelia laugh till she nearly choked! She mewed again, very loudly.

"Where *is* that cat!" cried the golliwog, in despair. "We've looked everywhere! Is he behind the curtain?"

"No, there's only Amelia Jane there!" said the curly-haired doll, looking. "There's no cat."

Well, of course, they didn't find any cat at all! And Amelia Jane didn't tell them it was she who had been mewing, so to this day they wonder where Tibs hid himself that night!

Then Amelia Jane saw a soda-water syphon left in a corner of the room. She knew how it worked, because she had seen Nurse using one. Oh, what fun it would be to squirt all the toys! She stole towards it—picked it up, and dear me, it *was* heavy! She ran at the surprised golliwog, pressed down the handle—and out gushed the soda-water all over him!

"Ow! Ooh!" he shouted, in

astonishment. "What is it! What is it! Amelia Jane, you ought to be ashamed of yourself!"

But she wasn't a bit ashamed. She was just enjoying herself thoroughly! She ran after the teddy bear and soaked him with soda-water too. She squirted lots over the clockwork mouse, and made him so wet that for two days his clockwork went wrong, and he couldn't be wound up. She squirted the pink rabbit, and he got into the wastepaper basket and couldn't get out, which worried him very much, because he was so afraid that Jane, the maid, would throw him away the next day! But she didn't, which was very lucky.

"Amelia Jane is up to her tricks again," said the clockwork clown, frowning. "We shall have no peace at all. What shall we do?"

"Take away her key!" said the clockwork mouse.

"She hasn't one, silly!" said the golly.

"Lock her in the cupboard!" said the teddy bear.

"She knows how to undo it from the inside," said the pink rabbit gloomily.

Nobody spoke for a whole minute. They were all thinking hard.

Then the clockwork clown gave a little laugh. "I know!" he said. "I've thought of an idea. It's quite simple, but it might work."

"What?" cried everyone.

"Let's polish Amelia Jane's shoes underneath and make them very, very slippery," said the clown. "Then, if she begins to run after us with soda-water syphons or things like that, down she'll go!"

"But she won't like that," said the curly-haired doll, who was rather tender-hearted.

"Well, *we* don't like the tricks she plays on *us*!" said the golly. "We'll do it, Clown! When she next takes her shoes off we'll polish them underneath till they are as slippery as glass!"

The very next night Amelia Jane took off her shoes because she said her feet were hot. She put the shoes into a corner and then danced round the nursery in her stockinged feet, enjoying herself. The clown picked up the shoes and ran away to the back of the toy

cupboard with them. He had a tiny
duster there, and a little bit of polish
he had taken out of Jane's polish jar
when the nursery had been cleaned out.
Aha, Amelia Jane, you'll be sorry for
all your tricks!

The clown polished and rubbed,
rubbed and polished. The soles of the
shoes shone. They were as slippery as

could be! The clown put them back and waited for Amelia Jane to put them on. This she very soon did, for she had stepped on a pin and pricked her foot! As she put her shoes on, she thought out a naughty trick!

"I'll run after all the toys with that pin I trod on!" she thought. "Oooh! That will make them rush away into all the corners! What fun it will be to frighten them!"

She buttoned her shoes and took the nasty long pin into her hand. Then she stood up and looked round, her naughty black eyes gleaming. "I'll run after that fat little teddy bear!" she thought. So off she went, straight at the teddy bear, holding the pin out in front of her.

"Amelia Jane, put that pin down!" shouted the teddy bear in fright—but before Amelia Jane had taken three steps, her very, very slippery shoes slid along the ground and down she fell, bumpity-bump! She *was* so surprised!

Up she got again and took a few more steps towards the teddy bear— but her shoes slipped and down she

fell! Bumpity-bump! She hit her head on the fender!

"What's the matter with the carpet?" cried Amelia Jane, in a rage. "It keeps making me fall down!"

"Ha ha! ho ho!" laughed the toys. "Perhaps there is slippery magic about, Amelia Jane!"

"Oh, I believe you toys have something to do with it!" shouted the angry doll. Up she got and took the pin in her hand again. "I'll show you what happens to people who put slippery magic on the floor! Here comes my pin!"

She tried to run at the golliwog, who was laughing so much that black tears ran all down his face. But down she went again, bumpity-bump—and oh my, the pin stuck into her knee! Yes, it really did—she fell on it!

How Amelia Jane squealed! How Amelia Jane wept! "Oh, the horrid pin! Oh, how it hurts!" she cried.

"Well, Amelia Jane, it serves you right," said the pink rabbit. "You were going to prick *us* with that pin and now it's pricked *you*! You know how it feels!"

Amelia Jane threw the pin away in a rage. The clown picked it up and flung it into the fire! He wasn't going to have pins about the nursery!

Amelia Jane got up again. "I'm going to bandage my knee where the pin pricked it," she said. She ran to the toy cupboard—but before she was half-way there, her slippery shoes slid away beneath her—and down she sat with a dreadful bumpity-bumpity-bump!

The toys laughed. Amelia Jane cried bitterly. The curly-haired doll felt sorry for her. "Don't cry any more, Amelia Jane," she said. "Take your shoes off and you won't fall again. We played a trick on you—but you can't complain because you have so often tricked *us*! You should not play jokes on other people if you can't take a joke yourself!"

Amelia Jane took her shoes off. She saw how the clown had polished them underneath, and she went very red. She knew quite well she could not grumble if people were unkind—because she too had been unkind.

"I'll try and be good, Toys," she

said at last. "It's difficult for me, because I'm not a shop-toy like you, so I haven't learnt good manners and nice ways. But I may be good one day!"

The toys thought it was nice of her to say all that. The curly-haired doll came to help her bandage her knee. The clown put a bandage round her head where she had bumped it. She looked so funny that they didn't know whether to laugh or cry at her.

Amelia Jane did enjoy being fussed! She was as nice as could be to the toys—but oh dear, oh dear, I do somehow feel perfectly certain that she can't be good for long!

CHAPTER III

AMELIA JANE AT THE SEA

ONCE it happened that Amelia Jane, the big, naughty doll, was taken down to the seaside with some of the other toys. The clockwork clown went, the brown teddy bear, the golliwog, and the golden-haired doll. They went in the car with the children, and they were all most excited.

"I shall dig in the sand and throw it over everybody!" said naughty Amelia Jane. "And I shall get my pail and fill it full of water and pour it down the golly's neck! Ho, won't he jump!"

"You'll do nothing of the sort, Amelia Jane," said the golliwog at once. "You know how often you've promised

to be good. Well, just you remember your promise."

"And I shall push the clockwork clown into a rock-pool and make him sit down there with all his clothes on," said Amelia Jane, with a naughty giggle.

"You mustn't!" cried the clown, in alarm. "If you do that, my clockwork

43

will get rusty and I shan't wind up properly—then I won't be able to walk any more, or turn head-over-heels!"

The children often took the toys down to the beach with them. After dinner the children went to have a rest, and the toys were left in a sheltered corner of the beach. No one ever came there, so the children knew they were quite safe. And it was whilst the toys were left alone there that Amelia Jane behaved so very badly. She did all she said she would, and more too.

She threw sand all over the golden-haired doll, and it went into her eyes dreadfully. She cried, and the golliwog had to find his handkerchief and comfort her. Whilst he was patting the doll on the back, and wiping the sand out of her eyes, Amelia Jane was filling her pail from a pool.

She crept up behind the golliwog— and tipped the pail of cold sea-water all down his black neck!

"Ooooo-ow-oooo!" yelled the golliwog, jumping about twelve inches into the air with fright. "You wicked doll,

Amelia Jane! I told you not to do that!"

Amelia Jane thought it was such a funny joke that she rolled over and over on the sand, laughing. The clockwork clown, who had seen all that had happened, remembered what she had said she would do to him, and he ran away to hide. He really was dreadfully afraid Amelia Jane would push him into a pool. Amelia looked for him. He had hidden himself under a clump of seaweed, so she couldn't see him—but she saw the brown teddy bear!

He was walking round the edge of a fine deep pool, looking at the crabs there. Amelia Jane crept up behind him. She gave him a push—SPLASH! The teddy landed in the pool and sat right down in the water.

"Oooooo-ow-ooooo!" he gasped, his mouth full of salty water. Amelia Jane laughed till the tears ran down her face.

"You are very naughty and unkind," said the clockwork clown, poking his head out of the seaweed nearby. "You are a most dreadful doll. Hi, Golly, come and help me push Amelia Jane into the water!"

"I shan't let you!" said Amelia Jane, at once. "I shall paddle out to sea and sit on that rock over there. I am bigger than any of you, and I can get through the deep water easily. You won't be able to follow me. I shall be quite safe. Ha ha to you, clockwork clown!"

Amelia Jane had no shoes or stockings on. She lifted up her red skirt and stepped into the waves. She waded out towards the big, big rock that showed itself some way out. It was covered with green sea-weed. The teddy shook the water from his fur and ran after Amelia, splashing through the waves. But he was afraid of getting drowned, and he soon came back. Amelia was a very big doll, so she could easily get to the rock. The water did not come to more than her knees.

She reached the rock and climbed up. She waved to the others.

"I'm the king of the castle!" she shouted, dancing on the rock. "You can't get me! I shall stay here and have a nice nap!"

She lay down on the soft green sea-weed. The hot sun had dried it well.

It was like a soft bed.

Amelia fell asleep. When the children came out to play, they didn't miss her. They had new spades and they wanted to dig a big castle.

They took no notice of any of the other toys, and didn't even see how wet the teddy bear was. They dug and dug and dug.

They had tea on the beach and then

they dug again. When it was time to go home they collected their toys and set off up the beach. They had the clockwork clown, the bear, the golliwog, and the golden-haired doll—but they didn't have Amelia Jane. They had forgotten all about her.

And what about Amelia Jane? She was still asleep on the rock! The tide was now coming in—and it crept higher and higher over the rock. Soon it would reach Amelia's toes. Soon a big wave would break right over the rock on top of Amelia—and then what would happen to her?

Amelia woke up. She sat up on the rock and looked round. When she saw how the tide was coming in, she was in a dreadful fright. The water was too deep to paddle through now. She couldn't swim. Oh dear!

Amelia Jane stood and yelled for help. "Save me, somebody!" she cried. "Save me!" But there was no one to save her. Poor Amelia Jane!

The other toys were sitting on a shelf, watching the children go to bed. Nobody thought of Amelia Jane. They were only too glad to forget her.

But when the children were safely in bed, the golliwog suddenly looked round—and saw no Amelia. For a moment he wondered where she was—and then he remembered! She had been left on the rock—and the tide was coming in. Oooooo!

"I say, Toys," said the golly, "Amelia Jane's on the rock—and the sea will soon cover it right over!"

Now you might think that the clown, the golden-haired doll, and the golly would say, "And serve Amelia right!" —but they didn't. They all looked at one another in alarm. Amelia was naughty—and she had played tricks on them—but they could not let anything horrid happen to her.

"What can we do?" asked the clown. He got down from the shelf and ran to the window. From there he could quite well see the rock on which Amelia stood, shouting for help.

"We must save her!" said the golden-haired doll.

"But how?" asked the golly.

"I know!" said the clown suddenly. "We will take the children's toy ship—

and sail it to the rock. We shall just get there in time. Hurry!"

The golly and the clown caught hold of the toy ship, which lay on the floor. They ran out of the door with the golden-haired doll, and tore down to the beach. They put the boat into the water.

The golly got in. The golden-haired doll got in. The clockwork clown pushed off, and then jumped in himself. The golly arranged the white sails so that the wind filled them. The clown took the rudder and guided the little ship.

The tide was coming in fast. It was a long, long way now to the rock. Amelia Jane was very frightened. A big wave had washed right over the rock and had wetted her to the waist. Amelia was afraid that the next one would wash her right off the rock into the big sea.

"Help! Help!" she shouted, as another big wave came over the rock. Amelia held on to some seaweed. The sea wetted her right up to her shoulders.

Oooh! It was so cold! She knew now how cold the golliwog must have felt when she poured water down his neck that morning!

"We're coming, Amelia Jane; we're coming!" shouted the toys. Amelia Jane heard them.

She looked over the waves and saw the three toys in the sailing-ship. It bobbed up and down as it came, for the sea was quite rough.

"Oh, you good creatures!" sobbed Amelia Jane. "I don't deserve to be rescued—I was so unkind to you—but oh, I'm *so* glad to see you!"

The ship sailed quite near to the rock. The clown was careful not to let it strike the rock—for that would mean a wreck. "Jump, Amelia, jump into the ship!" he called. "We can't come any nearer!"

Amelia Jane jumped. It was a good jump. She landed right in the middle of the boat. It swayed about, and then as the clown turned it into the wind, the sails filled and the little ship sailed towards the shore again.

"You'll soon be safe home," said the golden-haired doll kindly. "Don't cry, Amelia Jane."

"I won't tease you any more, any of you," wept Amelia. "It was so kind of you to remember I was on the rock and come to rescue me. Thank you ever and ever so much."

The ship reached the sand. The golly jumped out and pulled it in. The golden-haired doll jumped out and helped poor, wet, cold Amelia Jane out. The clown jumped out last of all—and then they carried the ship back to the nursery again.

The golly took Amelia Jane down to the kitchen fire and dried her. Then back to the nursery they went, and soon fell asleep after their exciting day.

And was Amelia Jane kinder to the toys after that? Yes, very much kinder, all the time they were away at the sea. But alas! When they went back home again, Amelia Jane forgot all her good ways. Read on and you will see!

CHAPTER IV

AMELIA JANE
AND THE COWBOY DOLL

NOW one day a funny little doll came to stay with the toys in the nursery. He was a cowboy doll. He didn't belong to the children who owned the nursery, he was just lent to them for a few days.

He was dressed in shaggy trousers, leather tunic, and a cowboy hat. He was very smart indeed, and the other toys were a bit afraid of him.

He could ride the old wooden horse, and made it gallop as fast as could be round and round the nursery! Once he even climbed up on to the big rocking-horse and made it rock so fast that the

horse hrrumphed in surprise, and Nurse came running in to see what all the noise was about!

The cowboy doll only just had time to hop off the horse and lie down on the floor, where he had been put by the children!

Another thing he could do was

rather marvellous. He had a long rope, and he could lasso anything with it that he liked! The toys would say to him, "Lasso that tree on the toy farm, Cowboy doll!" And he would quickly throw his looped rope, and the end would neatly curl round the tree and topple it over!

He would lasso anything, even a pin stuck in the floor. And then, of course, Amelia Jane began to tell him naughty things to do!

"Cowboy doll, do lasso the clock-work mouse!" she whispered. "Oh, do! Look, he is over there, sniffing at that brick!"

The cowboy doll grinned. He had a most wicked face. He threw his rope neatly, and the loop at the end dropped right over the mouse's head—click!

The mouse gave a squeak of surprise and tried to run away, but the rope held him tight! He was very frightened.

"You shouldn't tell the cowboy doll to do that, Amelia Jane," said the golliwog crossly. "Why *must* you always get into mischief? Go and untie the mouse, quickly."

"You go, Golly," said Amelia Jane, giggling as she thought of more mischief. "You are better at knots than I am!"

Well, the mouse was squealing so loudly that the golly really thought he had better go and help. So off he went, and Amelia Jane nudged the cowboy doll and whispered to him:

"Where's your other rope? Lasso

Golly! He will get such a shock!"

So when Golly was bending over the mouse, trying to undo the loop of rope round him, there came a whizzing noise through the air, and another rope fell neatly right round Golly's waist—click! It pinned his arms to his sides and he couldn't move! What a shock he got!

"You're my prisoner, Golly!" grinned the cowboy doll. "Come over here!"

"I won't!" scowled Golly. "Let me go!"

But he had to walk over to the cowboy doll and

Amelia Jane because the cowboy pulled hard at the rope, and Golly had to come with it! He was so angry!

Amelia Jane thought lassoing was a lovely thing to do. She wanted to learn, and the cowboy doll said he would teach her.

"No, you are not to teach her,"

said the golden-haired doll sharply. "She is quite naughty enough without learning any more tricks. You are NOT to teach her!"

But the cowboy doll was not used to obeying other people, so he took no notice at all. He began to teach Amelia Jane, and she tried very hard to learn.

Soon she could throw a rope wonderfully well, and then, what a time the poor toys had! They never knew when a rope was going to come whizzing through the air after them, falling over their heads and shoulders! It was most worrying.

Amelia Jane practised hard, but she could not get quite so good at it as the cowboy doll.

Once she sent the rope flying through

the air to catch the teddy bear as he walked along, and she missed him and got the rope round the chimney of the dolls' house.

Of course, she pulled too hard, and the chimney came off and fell on top of the bear's head. He was very cross indeed, and threw the chimney at Amelia Jane. She threw it back, and it hit the nursery cat on the nose. He was most surprised, and looked as if he would eat Amelia Jane. So she ran into the cupboard till the cat had gone down to the kitchen for his dinner.

The toys made her climb up to the dolls' house roof and put the chimney on again. She didn't like that at all, but she had to do it. But even then she wouldn't stop lassoing things.

She lassoed the humming-top when it was spinning and made it fall down in a fright. She threw her rope at a cow in the farmyard, but caught the farmer himself and jerked him so high in the air that he really thought he was flying. He came down in the coal-scuttle and was very angry about it. He told all his cows to go and bite Amelia Jane, and she had to climb up on to a shelf out of their way.

Another time she was very naughty indeed. She thought she would lasso Mister Noah, who lived in the wooden ark, and give him a shock. He didn't like Amelia Jane, and wouldn't even say good morning to her when he met her. So Amelia waited for him to come out with all his animals.

"I'll lasso him now!" she whispered
to the cowboy doll, with a grin. "Watch
me!"

She sent the rope through the air—
whizz! But she missed Mister Noah,
and the rope fell neatly round two tigers
and two bears! How they roared and
growled! They bit through the rope in
a twinkling, left the line of animals,

and tore over to where Amelia was standing with the cowboy doll.

The bears bit the cowboy doll so hard that they made a hole in his shaggy trousers. The tigers scratched Amelia Jane on her legs, and you should have heard her yell!

"It serves you right," said the golliwog, who had been watching. "We've told you ever so many times not to keep lassoing people."

So for a little while Amelia Jane was good, but then something happened that made her bad again.

Somebody left a bag of sweets on the nursery mantelpiece. They belonged to one of the children, and Nurse had put them there. Amelia Jane saw them and looked longingly at them, for she loved eating lots of sweets and chocolates.

How could she possibly get those sweets? She looked up at the mantelpiece and thought hard. The clock ticked away there. The goldfish globe winked back. It stood on the mantelpiece too, and was full of little black tadpoles that the children had found in the ponds. The china cat stood there too, watching the tadpoles wriggling about. And just by the cat was that bag of sweets.

"Oh, I know how I can get them!" said Amelia suddenly. "I can lasso them with the cowboy's rope! Cowboy doll, where are you? Will you lend me your rope for a moment?"

The cowboy doll untied it. He always kept it tied round his waist. He

gave it to Amelia Jane and asked her what she wanted it for.

"I'm going to lasso that bag of sweets on the mantelpiece and get it down here!" said naughty Amelia. "Then we'll share the sweets, Cowboy doll!"

"You'd better let *me* do the lassoing," said the cowboy. "You'll only go and lasso the cat or the clock, Amelia Jane!"

"No, *I* want to do it," said Amelia. She looked up at the mantelpiece and swung the rope carefully. Whizz! It flew up to the mantelpiece! It missed the bag of sweets. It missed the clock. It just missed the china cat, but it caught the goldfish bowl! It fell neatly round it. The rope was tight—it pulled at the bowl—it toppled it over!

The watching toys gave a shriek!

The water poured out of the bowl—all over Amelia and the cowboy doll, who were just underneath! Tadpoles fell down their necks and flopped on to the floor! The bowl fell off too, and all the toys thought it would smash on the floor.

But no! It was too clever for that! It fell on to Amelia Jane's head, and there she stood, wet through, with the glass bowl on her head like an extra big hat!

Well, really, the toys simply couldn't *help* laughing! She looked too funny, and the cowboy doll, too, was soaked from head to foot. He was trying to get a tadpole which had fallen down his back and was tickling him dreadfully.

"Don't stand there laughing like this," suddenly said the golly. "Those tadpoles will die out of water. Quick, get something to put them into."

The toys looked round for something but all they could think of was Amelia Jane's teacup. She was a big doll, so she had a very big cup. The toys put some water in it and then picked up the poor wriggling tadpoles. They found the one down the cowboy's neck, and took two from Amelia's neck as well. Dear, dear, what an excitement there was!

"What do you want to bother with silly tadpoles for, when Amelia Jane and I are all wet through!" cried the cowboy doll crossly. "Please dry us."

"It is more important to save the

tadpoles than to bother about *you*," said the clown. "You can dry yourselves. It was your own fault that all this happened. Amelia Jane had no right to try and lasso sweets that didn't belong to her!"

Amelia squeezed out her wet things and took the bowl off her head. It was rather a tight fit, and at first she thought she might have to wear the bowl all her life! That did give her a shock. She stood by the fire and tried to dry herself. She felt very cold and sad. The cowboy doll was wet too, and very angry.

"You *are* silly," he said to Amelia Jane. "Why didn't you let me do the lassoing? I could have got the bag of sweets then, but all we got was cold

water and tadpoles!"

Amelia Jane said nothing, but dear me, when she found that her teacup was full of swimming tadpoles she was horrified.

"How can I ever drink out of my nice cup again?" she wept. "It will be all tadpoley."

"Amelia Jane, stop being silly," said

the golliwog sternly. "You have made enough mischief without being stupid too. What do you suppose Nurse will say when she finds the tadpoles upset and the bowl on the rug?"

Nurse said a lot. She simply could *not* understand what had happened! At first she thought it was the cat who had done it. But no, Tibs had been in the kitchen all the time. And then she caught sight of the cowboy doll who was standing in a corner, still very wet.

"I believe it's you, with your lasso, you naughty doll!" she said. "Back you go to your own home!"

"Perhaps Amelia Jane will be good now that the cowboy doll has gone," said the teddy to the clown. But I don't expect she will—do you?

CHAPTER V
AMELIA JANE
AND THE PLASTICINE

NOW Amelia Jane had been good for a long time—so good that the golden-haired doll really wondered if Amelia was ill. But she wasn't ill; as the clown said, "She was just boiling up for some more mischief!"

Amelia Jane had found the box of plasticine in the cupboard, and every night she played with the plasticine. She sat in a corner by herself, and the other toys took no notice of her at all. Amelia Jane was clever with the plasticine—she could make flowers and shells and tables and chairs and all kinds of things, just as you can.

And then, of course, naughty ideas began to come into her mind. She had heard the teddy bear complaining that he had no tail. Suppose she made him one and stuck it on when he was asleep? He would think he had grown a tail, and what fun it would be to see him walking about proudly, showing off his beautiful new tail! What would he say when it came off?

Amelia Jane made a beautiful long tail of plasticine. It was brown to match the teddy bear's fur, and it had some pretty little blue spots here and there. Amelia Jane made some marks on it to make it look furry. It was finished at last. Amelia Jane grinned to herself and waited till she saw the teddy bear asleep in a corner.

Then she crept up to him with the plasticine tail. Nobody was about. Amelia Jane quickly pressed one end of the tail on to the teddy bear's back. It stuck nicely. Then the naughty doll ran back to her place in the cupboard.

Presently the clockwork clown walked along to talk to the bear. He

saw the tail, and he stared as if he couldn't believe his eyes!

"Hie, Teddy, Teddy, wake up!" he shouted in excitement. "You've grown a fine tail! You have really!"

The teddy woke up with a jump. When he saw his new tail, curling round him like a cat's, he was so surprised that he couldn't say a word at first. Then he got up and bent himself over to have a look at it.

"A tail at last!" he said. "A real tail! I always thought I might grow one, and now I have!"

"Golly, come and look at Teddy's beautiful new tail!" cried the clown. "Do come! It's a fine one!"

Golly came, and the golden-haired doll—and Amelia went too.

"It's magnificent," said Golly.

"It makes you look really handsome, Teddy," said the golden-haired doll.

"How clever of you to grow it all by yourself!" said naughty Amelia Jane.

"Wasn't it clever of me!" said Teddy proudly, and he walked about showing his new tail to every one. The clock-work mouse loved it, and the yellow duck said it was the longest she had ever seen. The bear was so happy that his boot-button eyes shone like lamps.

Not long afterwards the toys all sat down together to have cups of cocoa which the clockwork mouse had made for them on the stove in the dolls' house. Amelia Jane sat down beside the teddy—and whatever do you suppose she did? When the others were not looking she took hold of the bear's plasticine tail and with her clever fingers she made the end of it into a snake's head! Fancy that! It looked exactly like a snake now, with its mouth open and two little holes for eyes!

The golly saw it first and gave a shriek! "Oooh! Look! Your tail has

turned into a snake, Teddy!"

The bear looked down in alarm—
and when he saw the snake's head on
the end of his tail he jumped up with a
yell.

"Oh! Go away, snake, go away!"
he shouted, and he ran to the other side
of the room. But, of course, his tail
followed him, for it was stuck on to
him—and it looked as if the snake was

running after him backwards! Poor Teddy! He was so frightened. He didn't like snakes at all, and to have his new tail turning into one seemed very dreadful to him.

Well, Amelia Jane laughed till she cried. It seemed so funny to her to see the teddy bear rushing about with a snake-tail! The toys thought her very unkind to laugh, and the golden-haired doll slapped her. But as Amelia Jane could slap twice as hard, that wasn't much good!

"Take your tail off, silly, if you're afraid of it!" called Amelia Jane.

"How can you take off a thing that's growing on you, stupid!" yelled back the teddy.

Amelia Jane ran to the bear and

jerked at his tail. It came off quite easily, of course, for it was only plasticine. She threw it out of the window. The toys looked on in surprise. Then they all cheered Amelia.

"How brave of you, Amelia Jane! How good of you to do that! Did it hurt, Teddy?"

"Not a bit," said Teddy, in surprise. "Oh, thank you, Amelia Jane. The snake might have bitten you. You are very brave."

Amelia Jane didn't tell the toys that the tail had only been plasticine made by herself. No—the naughty doll said nothing at all, but let the toys make a fuss of her.

"I'll think of another plasticine trick," she thought gleefully. And, as you can guess, it wasn't very long before she did!

She made a set of nice little chairs, all with seats and backs and four neat little legs. Then she went to the paintbox and got the red paint. She painted those little chairs a bright red, and really, they looked simply lovely when she had finished. But, of course, you couldn't sit down on them because they were only made of plasticine and would crumple up at once!

But they didn't look as if they were made of plasticine when they were bright red. They looked like wooden chairs. Amelia Jane set them all out neatly in the middle of the floor.

"What are those chairs for?" asked the golly, in surprise.

"I'm going to have a party," said Amelia Jane, and she got a table from the dolls' house. Then she called to the toys, "Do come and join my party. The cakes haven't come yet but they'll be here soon. Just come and sit down and wait a while, Toys!"

The toys were pleased, for they loved any sort of a party. They came running over to Amelia Jane. Even the clockwork mouse came, and so did the old blue rabbit who had only one eye and no whiskers at all.

"Do sit down," said Amelia, waving her hand to the red chairs. "I hope there are enough seats for you all!"

Every one sat down—but oh, what a shock they got! The golly's chair sank down at once, all its legs broken! He landed with such a bump on the ground! The golden-haired doll's chair tipped over backwards, and she bumped her head, and sat so hard on the plasticine that it stuck to her pretty blue frock. The clockwork mouse's chair crumpled up and he fell off and lost his key.

One by one all the red chairs gave way and tipped out the surprised toys.

The clown didn't know what was happening and he clutched the back of his chair so hard that he squeezed up the plasticine it was made of and got it all over his arms! What a shock for him!

Amelia Jane thought it was so funny! She laughed and laughed and laughed.

"It isn't funny," said the golly angrily. "Is this a trick instead of a party?"

"Yes," said Amelia Jane. "Oh, Golly you did look funny tumbling on to the floor!"

"I suppose there are no cakes coming after all," said the clown fiercely. "And

I suppose too that it was you who stuck on the teddy bear's tail, and made it of plasticine! You are a wicked doll and you deserve to be frightened yourself!"

"Oh, you can't frighten me!" said Amelia Jane. "I'm not afraid of anything!"

But she was, you know—she was afraid of black beetles! The toys knew this, and they made up their minds to punish her! They went to the plasticine box, and the clown, who was clever with his fingers made lots of big beetles, all with feelers on their heads and six legs under their bodies! The clown painted them black.

"This isn't a very kind thing to do," said the clown, as he finished the last beetle, "but really, Amelia Jane is so naughty that we must teach her a lesson. Where is she?"

"In the toy cupboard, reading," said the mouse. The clown took up the black beetles and put them here and there on the floor. Then he called Amelia Jane.

"Amelia, Amelia, come quickly!"

Amelia Jane put down her book and rushed out of the cupboard—but when she saw those black plasticine beetles she gave such a yell!

"Oooh! Ow! Beetles! Where have they come from! Take them away!"

The bear had tied a bit of black cotton to one beetle and he suddenly jerked this. The beetle jumped, and Amelia Jane screamed: "It's coming after me! It's coming after me! Oooooooh!"

She rushed back into the toy cupboard and crouched in the darkest corner. And do you know, she didn't come out of the cupboard for two days, so the toys had a lovely time playing together without wondering what mischief Amelia Jane was up to!

They have taken away the black beetles, of course, but Amelia Jane doesn't know that! She'll think twice before she gets into mischief again, won't she!

CHAPTER VI

STOP IT, AMELIA JANE!

YOU might think that Amelia Jane would grow out of her bad ways, but she didn't. The day soon came when she felt bad again. It was the day that the pop-gun came to the nursery. The children had bought it and had been playing with it. It was great fun.

It was a wooden gun that had a cork fitted in at the end of it. When you pressed the trigger the cork flew out with a pop, but it didn't go far, because

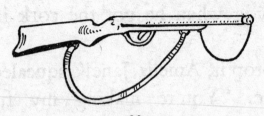

it was tied on to the gun with a piece of string. The children set up their wooden soldiers in a row and shot them down—bang!—with the pop-gun. The soldiers didn't mind, because it was what they were made for.

But when Amelia Jane got hold of the pop-gun that night and began shooting the cork at every one, there was trouble!

"Stop it, Amelia Jane!" shouted the clockwork clown angrily, when his cap flew off into the coal-scuttle, shot there by the cork.

"Stop it, Amelia Jane!" cried the golliwog when he got the cork in his eye.

"Stop it, Amelia Jane!" squealed the engine. "You're making my funnel

loose with that cork—it keeps hitting it!"

But do you suppose Amelia Jane stopped? Of course not! She was enjoying herself far too much!

She shot at the castle of bricks and down they all fell! She shot at everything in the toy farmyard, and trees, animals, and farmer fell over flat. She shot at the clockwork mouse and gave him such a fright that he ran into the dolls' house and hid under a bed. Nobody could get him out.

The clockwork clown called the other toys to him. "We've got to stop Amelia Jane!" he said. "I'm tired of all this popping. That cork doesn't do much damage but it stings all the same."

"What about shooting Amelia Jane?" asked the golliwog eagerly. "I'd like to do that."

"Oh, she won't let that pop-gun go, you may be sure of that!" said the teddy bear.

"Well, there's a funny old gun in the cupboard that the children got out of a cracker," said the clockwork clown.

"Why not shoot at her with that?"

"Because it doesn't shoot, silly," said the bear. "I've tried it heaps of times."

"If it only made a pop it would do," said the clown gloomily. "We don't really want to shoot Amelia Jane—only to frighten her and make her stop popping the cork-gun at us."

"Well, that old gun doesn't shoot and it doesn't make a pop either," said the golliwog.

Then the bear had an idea. "Listen!" he whispered, so that Amelia Jane wouldn't hear. "I know where there is a packet of balloons! Couldn't we get them—and blow them up—and let Golly hide behind the curtain with them? Then I could hold the gun and point it at Amelia Jane—and at the same moment

Golly would prick a balloon and burst it! Then it would go—*bang!* just like a gun—and frighten Amelia Jane!"

Every one thought that was a splendid idea. So the golly got the packet of balloons and went behind the curtain to blow them up. There were five. The bear found the gun and polished it up. Amelia Jane saw him and laughed.

"*That* old gun won't shoot!" she said, and she aimed the pop-gun at Teddy and shot the cork so hard that one of his ears went crooked. He was very angry.

"Oh, so you think this old gun won't shoot!" he said. "Well, you're wrong!"

He pointed the gun at Amelia Jane— and at the same moment Golly dug a pin into one of the blown-up balloons

he had behind the curtain.

"Bang!" went the balloon—and Amelia Jane gave a shriek. She really thought the gun that Teddy was holding had gone off!

"I'm shot! I'm shot!" yelled Amelia Jane in a fright. Every one laughed. Teddy pointed the gun at the naughty

99

doll again. "Bang!" went another balloon behind the curtain. Amelia Jane squealed and ran away.

"I'm shot again! I'm shot again!" she yelled. Teddy laughed so much that he nearly dropped the gun.

"Do you promise not to shoot anybody with that pop-gun again?" he said.

"No, I don't!" said Amelia Jane.

"All right then!" said Teddy, and he pointed the gun at her again. "I'll go on shooting at *you* then."

"Bang!" went a third balloon behind the curtain, and Amelia Jane screamed, "I'm shot! I'm shot! He's shot me three times!"

"Bang!" went another balloon, and "Bang!" went the fifth balloon. Amelia

Jane screamed so loudly that she quite deafened every one. She fled into the toy cupboard and wept bitterly.

"I won't shoot any one any more. Here's the old pop-gun!" she cried and she threw it out of the cupboard to the teddy bear. "Stop shooting me! I'm wounded everywhere!"

When Amelia Jane next came out of the toy cupboard the toys stared in astonishment— for the big doll had bandaged her arms and legs and head. She did look funny!

"You shot me five times and wounded me," said Amelia Jane in a hurt voice. "You ought to be very sorry."

But the toys laughed and laughed and laughed. How could she be wounded when it was only balloons that went off pop and not the gun? Oh, Amelia Jane, you are just a humbug!

CHAPTER VII
AMELIA JANE UP THE CHIMNEY

INTO the nursery where naughty Amelia Jane lived, came a little black kitten one day. Its eyes were green, its tail was fat and long, and its little paddy-paws were like velvet.

All the toys loved the kitten at once —but Amelia Jane loved it most of all! How she cuddled it! How she fussed it! How she stroked it from ears to tail-tip and tickled it under its soft black chin!

The kitten belonged to the cook. It was a pretty, gentle little thing, and it let the toys do what they liked with it. The teddy found it a buttery crumb to nibble. The clockwork clown turned head over heels seven times running to make it laugh. The golliwog found the dolls' hair-brush and brushed its fur till it shone.

But Amelia Jane wanted the kitten all to herself. She pushed away the other toys, and as she was bigger than they were they fell down, flop! That was the worst of Amelia—she was always so rough!

"*I* want this kitten!" said Amelia Jane. "Tiddles, Tiddles, purr to me, and to no one else!"

"You are very selfish, Amelia Jane," said the golliwog. Amelia Jane stuck out her elbow and pushed him again. Down he went, flip-flop! You couldn't do anything with Amelia Jane when she was feeling like that.

"This kitten is mine when it comes into our nursery," said Amelia. "Nobody else is to play with it then."

Well, the kitten quite enjoyed being made a fuss of by Amelia, but it did want to play with the other toys sometimes. Amelia just wouldn't let it. She caught it and put it on her knee to

stroke as soon as ever it ran over to Golly or Teddy.

And one day Amelia Jane thought she would like to dress the kitten up in clothes out of the dolls' chest-of-drawers! Quite a lot of clean dolls' clothes were kept there. It was really rather exciting to pull open the drawers and see the dear little coats and dresses, the fussy little bonnets with ribbons on, the socks and the shoes of all colours!

Amelia Jane pulled out the whole lot. She would, of course!

"Just look at that!" groaned Golly. "Untidy creature! She'll never put those clothes back again neatly. *We* shall have to do that!"

Amelia Jane soon had all the clothes on the floor. She wondered which would fit the little black kitten. What fun to dress her up, she thought!

"This dress will fit you nicely, Tiddles," she said, picking up a little red frock. "Oh, you will look sweet in it. And this yellow coat will fit you, too —and this little bonnet with ribbons! Oh, what a darling kitten you will look!"

"Mee-ow," said Tiddles, not at all liking the idea of being dressed up by Amelia Jane. "Mee-ow! I'm off!"

She shot to the nursery door—but Amelia Jane was too quick. She reached out her hand and caught poor Tiddles by the tail. "You come here!" she said. "I'm going to make you look really sweet!"

Well, Tiddles had to sit and be

dressed up. First Amelia put on the little red frock and did all the buttons up the back. Then she put on the yellow coat. She tied a ribbon round Tiddles' waist. Then she put the bonnet on Tiddles' little black head and tied it on firmly.

"There!" she said. "You are now a little dolly cat! You look lovely! Look, everybody!"

Everybody came to look. They couldn't help thinking that Tiddles really did look rather sweet—but Tiddles hated it! She struggled and wriggled and tried her hardest to scrape off her bonnet. She didn't like anything over her ears. She couldn't hear properly.

"Now, you shall look at yourself in the glass, Tiddles," said Amelia Jane, and she carried the dressed-up kitten to the big looking-glass.

The kitten looked at herself—and when she saw herself looking so very strange, with a bonnet on her ears, and a coat and dress hiding her black fur, she was afraid.

"Mee-ow! It isn't me!" she said in

a fright, and she rushed away to go downstairs to Cook. But Amelia Jane pushed the door shut.

"You're not to go away, Tiddles," she said. "We want to see you walking about nicely in your new clothes."

But that was just what Tiddles couldn't and wouldn't do! She caught sight of herself in the glass again and ran off in terror. She was so frightened that she meant to get out of the nursery somehow! But how could she? The door was shut. The window was shut.

"Oh, where can I go-ee-ow?" mewed poor Tiddles.

Now it was summer-time, so there was no fire in the nursery grate. Tiddles leapt over the guard, and in a trice she scrabbled up the chimney and was gone!

The toys stared at one another in alarm. What would happen to Tiddles up the chimney?

"Are you all right, Tiddles?" called the golliwog, sticking his black head up the chimney.

"No-ee-oh-ee-ow!" wailed poor Tiddles, who was more frightened than ever up the dark chimney. She didn't dare to go up and she didn't dare to go down! Poor Tiddles!

The toys turned fiercely on naughty Amelia Jane. "It's your fault!"

shouted Teddy. "You would dress her up and frighten her, just to amuse yourself. Now what are we to do?"

"Oh-ee-ow-ee-oh!" wailed Tiddles, up the chimney.

" I know! We'll make Amelia Jane go up the chimney and fetch Tiddles!" cried the golliwog. "That's what we'll do!"

"I won't go," said Amelia Jane.

"Oh yes, you will!" said Teddy. "Come on, every one. Push Amelia up the chimney!"

But they couldn't get the big doll to go. She just wouldn't be pushed. Just as the toys were going to have another push at Amelia, some one opened the nursery door. It was Cook!

The toys at once lay down flat

on the floor and kept quite still.

"I wonder where that kitten of mine is," said Cook, looking round the nursery. "I thought I heard her mewing up here."

"Oh-ee-ow-ee-ow!" wailed Tiddles from the chimney. Cook looked astonished. "I believe she's up the chimney!" she said. Then some one called her from downstairs and she hurried away.

Now Amelia Jane, although she really was a very naughty doll, was feeling most uncomfortable about poor Tiddles, for she was fond of her. As soon as the cook had gone she ran across to the fireplace, climbed over the guard, and looked up the chimney.

"I'm going up the chimney to rescue Tiddles," she said to the surprised toys.

"I'm not going because you tried to push me up—I'm going because I don't like Tiddles to be frightened."

And up the chimney went Amelia Jane! The toys listened to her scrabbling her way up the long, dark, sooty chimney. Bits of soot fell down and one bit hit the teddy on the nose. "The chimney wants sweeping," he said.

"Looks as if Amelia is sweeping it!" said the golliwog, as another bit of soot rolled down.

At last Amelia Jane reached Tiddles who sat in a sooty corner, trembling. Amelia Jane put her arm round the kitten and hugged her. "I'll help you to get down," she said.

But dear me, that wasn't easy! Amelia Jane lost her way in the chimney, which

joined all sorts of other chimneys here and there! Tiddles clung to her with all her claws and Amelia felt as if she was being pricked with twenty needles!

Now, very soon, Cook came into the nursery again, and who do you suppose was with her? The sweep! Yes—Cook had told him a kitten was up the chimney, and he had said he would try to sweep her out very gently.

He screwed on the handles of his big brush one after another, and the brush went higher and higher up the chimney. Amelia Jane heard it coming. She didn't know the chimney was being swept. The toys had all rushed into the cupboard when they heard Cook and the sweep coming upstairs! They hadn't had time to tell her anything.

"Oooh! What's this coming up the chimney?" suddenly said Amelia, as she dimly saw something black and hairy coming nearer and nearer. She didn't know it was the sweep's round black brush! "Oooh! It's got whiskers! It's touched me! It's pushing me!"

Poor Amelia Jane! She was just as

frightened as the kitten had been when it first ran up the chimney! She couldn't get away from the brush. It lifted her and the kitten up, up, and up!

"It's caught me, it's caught me!" wept Amelia. "I didn't know a whiskery thing lived in chimneys!"

The brush swept Amelia Jane and the kitten right out of the chimney into the air! The kitten fell to the roof on its feet, and made its way carefully down to the kitchen, where the cook took off the dolls' clothes in much astonishment.

Amelia didn't fall on *her* feet, because she wasn't a cat but a doll! She slid down the roof. She hung for a moment in the gutter. She fell over the gutter—down down, down—and into the prickly holly bush that grew just below!

"Oooh-ee-ow-ee-ooh!" yelled Amelia, for the holly bush pricked her well! She scrambled out somehow and after a long time got back to the nursery.

But when she crept in at the door, what a fright she gave the toys! She was blacker than a golliwog! Her clothes were sooty and torn! Her face and arms were pricked and scratched!

"Oooooh!" yelled the toys and rushed to shut themselves in the cupboard. "What is it? What is it?"

"It's me, Amelia Jane," said Amelia, in a very small voice. "I've come back."

"Well, you look DREADFUL!" said Teddy, sticking his head out of the cupboard. "For goodness' sake undress and have a bath and put on clean clothes!"

So Amelia did—but the clothes in the dolls' chest were much too small for her, and she did look funny walking about in things belonging to the baby doll!

"I shall be good in future," said Amelia Jane. But I don't believe it, do you?

CHAPTER VIII
AMELIA JANE AND THE SOAP

AMELIA JANE was feeling very bored. She had behaved herself for a whole week!

"But only because she hasn't been able to think of anything naughty to do," said Golly to Teddy. "As soon as she thinks of something she'll cheer up and be as bad as ever."

Well, it wasn't long before Amelia Jane did cheer up. She had thought of something.

You see, it was like this—she had gone out for a nice walk, sitting in the dolls' pram, and she had been taken into the town. Now, racing up and down the pavement were two boys on roller-skates. What a pace they went!

Amelia Jane leaned out of the pram to watch them. She thought it was a lovely game. She tried to see what the boys had on their feet, but they went so fast that Amelia Jane really didn't see what the skates were like.

"How *do* they slip along so fast?" she thought. "I *would* like to skate like that. How I wish I could! I'd go round and round the nursery, and down the passage and back. My, wouldn't the toys stare!"

Now, when Amelia Jane had an idea she just had to carry it out. So when she got back to the nursery she sat at the back of the toy cupboard and thought hard.

"I want to skate," she said to herself. "I want to put something on my feet and slip along like those boys. I want to go fast! But what can I put on my feet?"

"What are you thinking so hard about?" asked the clockwork clown, poking his head in at the door.

"Never you mind," said Amelia Jane.

"Tell me, and maybe I can help," said the clown.

"Well, I'm trying to think of something nice and slippery," said Amelia Jane.

"What about jelly?" said the clown.

"Don't be silly," said Amelia.

"Well, soap," said the clown. "Nice wet soap! Why, the other day I got hold of some wet soap and squeezed it—and it shot out of my hand like lightning and hit the golliwog on the ear!"

Amelia Jane laughed. Then she stopped and thought quickly. Soap! Yes—that was really a *good* idea! If she got two nice pieces of soap, made them wet and slippery and tied them under her feet, she would be able to slip along just like those boys on skates! Good!

"I'll try it!" said Amelia Jane. So she ran out of the toy cupboard and went to the nursery basin. She climbed up and looked to see if there was any soap there. There was—and what luck! —it had broken into two nice pieces.

"Oooh!" said Amelia, in delight. "Just what I want!"

She turned on the tap and wetted the soap till it was so slippery she could hardly hold it. Then she climbed down with it. The toys looked at her in amazement.

"What are you going to do?" said

Teddy. "Are you going to give yourself a good wash for once?"

"Don't be rude," said Amelia. "You'll see in a minute what I'm going to do."

She took off her hair-ribbon and tore it in two. Naughty Amelia! Then she tied one piece of soap under her right foot and the other piece under her left foot. The toys stared at her as if they thought she was mad.

"Amelia, that's a funny way of washing your feet," said Golly at last.

"I'm not washing my feet. I'm going to *skate*!" said Amelia proudly. "Turn back the carpet, somebody. I must skate on the polished floor."

The toys began to giggle. Really, what *would* Amelia Jane do next! Teddy and Golly turned back the carpet. Unfortunately they rolled the clockwork mouse up in it and had to unroll it again to get him out.

"Oh, do be quick!" said Amelia impatiently. "I am simply longing to begin!"

At last the carpet was rolled right back. Amelia Jane began. She put first one foot out—slid along a little way on the soap—then put the other foot forward and slid too—and before the toys knew what she was about, there she was, skating round the nursery on her soap-skates!

How the toys laughed! Really, it was too funny to see Amelia sliding along so fast on pieces of soap!

Amelia Jane tried to stop—but she toppled and fell over, bang! The toys

roared. It was funny to watch Amelia sitting down, plop, glaring at them angrily.

"How dare you laugh at me!" cried Amelia Jane. "I shall go and learn how to skate in the passage. There is a nice polished linoleum there—I shall slide beautifully!"

"No, stay here," said the clown, in alarm. "You know quite well that somebody may go along that passage and see you, Amelia Jane."

"Pooh, every one's in bed," said Amelia, and this was true, for it was past midnight. "Anyway, you won't be able to laugh at me there, if I fall down—for none of you dares to come into the passage."

It was dark in the passage, for only a

small light burnt there. Amelia slid out on her soap-skates and began to slide gaily up and down, up and down! The kitchen cat, hearing the noise, came creeping up the stairs, wondering if there was an extra-large-size mouse anywhere about.

He *was* astonished when he saw Amelia. He ran along the passage to see what she had on her feet. Amelia didn't hear him or see him, and she suddenly bumped right into him. Crash! She fell over and banged her head against the bedroom door.

"Sh! Amelia Jane! Sh!" whispered the golly, putting his head out of the nursery door. But Amelia Jane wouldn't hush. She got up angrily and smacked the cat on its black nose. The cat spat and hissed, which scared her a bit.

If Amelia Jane had been sensible she would have run back to the nursery at once, but she was so keen on skating that she once more began to slide up and down, up and down, all along the passage. She didn't hear Nurse's bed creaking. She didn't hear Nurse creeping to the door. She didn't even see Nurse poking her head round the door—no, she went slipping and sliding up and down on the soap, having a perfectly lovely time!

Nurse couldn't make out who or what it was, for the passage was so dark. But she could quite well see something going up and down the passage, skating quickly. She moved to the light switch to put a brighter light on.

Amelia Jane saw her then. Quick as lightning the doll slipped through the nursery door, fell over on the carpet, tore off the bits of soap, and ran to the toy cupboard. She climbed in on top of the bear and the clown, who were very angry at being walked on.

But nobody dared to say a word! Suppose Nurse had seen what was happening? But when Nurse turned on the big light, all she saw was the kitchen cat sitting calmly by the wall.

"Good gracious," she said, "so it was *you* I saw, Puss, skating up and down the passage! What do you mean by doing that in the middle of the night, I should like to know! My goodness, what is the world coming to, when cats take to sliding up and down passages and waking everybody up! Shoo! Shoo!"

She shooed the cat down the stairs, and he disappeared quickly, tail in air, boiling with rage to think that Amelia Jane had slipped off and left him to take the blame.

And in the morning, when Nurse saw the messy bits of soap lying on the carpet, she was crosser than ever.

"Just look at that!" she said to Jane, the housemaid. "It must be that cat. Slipped and slid down the passage all night long like a mad thing—and then went and tried to eat the soap out of the basin! I'll spank it well!"

She did. Poor Puss! Amelia Jane laughed to hear him yowl—but she didn't laugh quite so much when the cat came upstairs and tore her new dress with his sharp claws.

"You'd better not skate any more with the soap, Amelia Jane," said the golly. "It's funny to watch you—but if you get other people into trouble it's not fair!"

So that was the end of Amelia Jane skating on the soap. I would have loved to see her, wouldn't you?

CHAPTER IX

AMELIA JANE AND THE SNOW

IT was snowing hard. The toys looked out of the nursery window and watched the big white snowflakes come floating down.

"The garden has a new white carpet," said the teddy bear.

"Let's send the clockwork clown out to sweep the dust off it!" said Amelia Jane, the big naughty doll, with a giggle.

"Don't be silly, Amelia," said the clown. "You do say stupid things. There's no dust on a snow-carpet!"

"Isn't it pretty!" said the pink rabbit. "I'd like to go and burrow in it!"

"Let's go and play in it!" said the

curly-haired doll. "It would be such fun."

"Come on, then!" said Amelia Jane. She ran to the door, peeped out, and beckoned the others. "Nobody's about. We'll slip out of the garden-door and go to the bit of garden behind the hedge. Nobody will see us there."

"Stop a bit, Amelia Jane," said the clockwork clown. "Put on a coat. It's very cold outside."

"Pooh!" said Amelia impatiently. "Don't be such a baby, clockwork clown! I shall be as warm as toast running about. I'm going!"

She ran off down the stairs. But the other toys stayed to put on hats, coats, and scarves. Even the clockwork mouse put a red handkerchief round his neck.

When they got out to the snow they found that Amelia Jane had already made herself a great many snowballs! She danced about as they came, and shouted in glee.

"Let's have a snow-fight! Come on! I've got my snowballs ready. Look out, clown! Look out, pink rabbit!"

The big doll threw a snowball hard. It hit the clown on the head and he fell over, plonk! Amelia Jane giggled. She threw a snowball at the curly-haired doll and hit her in her middle. The doll gave a squeal and sat down in the snow.

"Ooh, this is fun!" yelled Amelia. "Come on, every one, get some snowballs ready!"

But nobody could make such big hard snowballs as Amelia Jane. Amelia

did enjoy herself. She pelted all the toys with snowballs, hitting them on the head and the chest and the legs— anywhere she could. She was quite a good shot, and the toys got very angry.

"Amelia Jane! Stop!" shouted the golliwog. "It isn't fair. Your snowballs are three times as big as ours, and you make them so hard that they hurt. Stop, I tell you!"

But Amelia Jane wouldn't stop. No, she went on and on—and how she laughed when all the toys turned and ran away from her shower of snowballs!

"Let's leave her alone," said the clown crossly. "She's too tiresome for anything."

"But she'll follow us and go on snowballing us," said the mouse.

"No, she won't. She's found something else to snowball," said the teddy bear. "Look! She's snowballing the kitten!"

So she was. The kitten didn't mind the snowballs at all because she could always dodge them. She pounced on them as they fell, and Amelia Jane laughed to see her. She forgot about the toys.

"What shall we do?" said the curly-haired doll.

"Let's build a nice, round snow-house," said the clown eagerly. "It would be such fun to do that. I know

how to. You just pile nice hard snow round in a ring and gradually make a round wall higher and higher. Then you make the wall slope inwards till the sides meet, and that's the roof!"

"Oh yes, that would be lovely!" said the golliwog. "We could all live in the snow-house then."

"But we won't let Amelia Jane come in at all," said the clockwork mouse, getting a little snowball for the wall of the house.

"No, we won't," said the curly-haired doll. "It will punish her for throwing such hard snowballs at us."

The toys worked hard at their snow-house. Soon the wall was quite high. It was a perfectly round wall. It grew higher and higher—and at last, as the toys shaped it to go inwards, the round sides met together and made a rounded roof.

The toys made a dear little doorway at the bottom. They were very excited, for the house was lovely. The clown ran to the pond, cut a square piece of ice, and ran back with it.

"What's that for?" asked the pink rabbit.

"A window, of course!" said the clown. He made a square hole in the side of the house and fitted in the piece of ice. It made a lovely window!

"Now let's go inside and be cosy," said the curly-haired doll. So they all crowded into the dear little snow-house and sat down. It was lovely.

But just as the clockwork clown was telling a nice story, Amelia Jane came up. The kitten had gone indoors, and Amelia Jane wanted some one else to play with. She had looked and looked for the toys, but as they were in the snow-house she hadn't seen them.

She suddenly saw the house and came running up to it. She peeped inside the window.

"Oh, what a nice little house!" she

cried. "Let me come in, too!"

"No, Amelia Jane!" shouted all the toys. "You are too big. Besides, we don't want you."

"But I'm very, very cold," said Amelia Jane, and certainly she was shivering.

"Well, you should have been sensible and put on your coat and hat as we did!" said the curly-haired doll.

"Oh, *do* let me come in!" begged Amelia, who hated to be left out of anything. "Oh, do let me!"

"NO, NO, NO!" shouted the toys.

"Well, I'm *coming* in!" said Amelia crossly, and she began to push her way in at the door. A bit of the doorway fell down at once.

"Don't!" cried the clown, in alarm.

"You will break our house!"

"Serve you right!" said naughty Amelia. But the toys really couldn't bear to see their house broken.

"All right, all right, you can come in," said the golliwog. "But wait till we get out, Amelia. You are so big that there isn't room for any one else when *you're* inside!"

That pleased Amelia very much. She thought it would be lovely to have the house all to herself. She waited until all the toys had squeezed out of the house, and then she went in.

"Oh, it's lovely!" she cried. She pressed her nose to the window and looked out. "It's lovely! It's a real little house. This shall be mine. You build another one for yourselves, Toys."

But the toys were tired. They stared angrily at Amelia Jane.

"You are a very naughty, selfish doll," shouted the teddy bear. "First you snowball us till we have to run away. Then you take our house for your own."

"I'm cold," said the clown, shivering. "Let's go and slide on the ice for a bit. Perhaps Amelia will get tired of our house soon and we can have it again."

So they went off to the pond and left Amelia Jane by herself.

Amelia felt cold. She shivered and shook in the little snow-house. "I wish there was a fire in this house," she said to herself, "then it would be nice and warm. I'll make one! How the toys will stare when they see I have a nice fire to warm myself by! But I shan't let them come in at all!"

She ran to the wood-shed and got some wood. She found some matches there that the gardener used when he lighted a bonfire. She ran back to the snow-house. Soon the twigs were crackling loudly.

"What's that noise?" said the clown

suddenly. All the toys stopped their sliding and listened. It came from their snow-house.

"Amelia Jane is lighting a fire there!" said the golliwog. Then the toys looked at one another—and began to giggle. They knew quite well what would happen if any one lighted a fire in a house made of snow! They ran up to watch.

"You can't come in, you can't come in!" shouted Amelia Jane. "This is my house, and this is my own dear little warm fire! Oh, I'm so cosy! Oh, I'm so warm!"

The toys stood and watched. The fire blazed up as the twigs burnt. There was a red glow inside the little house. It certainly looked very cosy. Amelia Jane put out her hands and warmed them inside the house.

But something was happening. The fire was melting the house! After all, it was only made of snow! The walls began to drip. The roof began to drip. The bit of ice that was the window disappeared altogether.

Amelia Jane felt the drips on her back and was cross.

"Who's pouring water on me?" she cried. "Stop it, or I'll be very angry!"

Drip, drip, drip went the snow as it melted all around her. And suddenly the whole house fell in, for the snow was now so soft and melty that it couldn't hold together. The fire went out with a sizzle.

Amelia Jane disappeared, for the snow fell all over her!

"Oooh! Ow! What's happened?" yelled Amelia Jane, very frightened. She kicked about in the wet snow, and first her hands came out, and then her head. She sat in the snow and looked around.

"Ha ha! Ho ho ho!" roared the toys. "It serves you right, Amelia Jane! You took our house—and you lighted a fire

and melted it—and it fell on top of you! Ha ha! Ho ho ho!"

Amelia Jane began to cry. She was wet through and very cold. She ran back to the nursery, leaving little wet marks all the way. She sat by the fire there and tried to get dry.

And very soon she began to sneeze: "A-tishoo! A-tishoo!"

"Now I've got a cold!" she said miserably. "Oh, why do I get naughty? Something nasty always happens to me when I do!"

"Well, just try and remember that, next time you feel naughty," said the golliwog, giving Amelia his big red handkerchief.

But I don't expect she'll remember it, do you?

CHAPTER X

AMELIA JANE GOES MAD

ONCE, when Amelia Jane, that big rascal of a doll, had been good for simply ages, she suddenly got tired of it and went quite mad! Never in her life had she been so naughty and, really, the toys got quite scared of her!

She was quite silly over water. She thought it was the greatest fun to fill the watering-can that belonged to the children, and lie in wait for any toy to come by at night.

She hid behind the curtain and waited till the golliwog came by. Then she tilted up the little green can and watered him! Goodness, how he jumped!

"It's raining!" he cried, and ran to get his umbrella. But when he put it up, no rain fell at all, and every one laughed at him.

"It never rains in the nursery, silly!" said the clockwork clown.

"Well, look at my wet hair," said the golliwog, and he shook a shower of drops all over the clown. "What do you call that if it isn't rain?"

The clockwork clown snorted, and went to visit the clockwork mouse over in the corner. He didn't know that Amelia Jane was hiding behind the scuttle with the watering-can again! Just as he came by, whistling a merry little tune, Amelia tilted up the can—and, pitter-patter! down came the water over the startled clown.

He ran to get the umbrella then— and holding it carefully over him, he

went back to the scuttle to find out
what the water was. And there, of
course, he found Amelia, laughing till
the tears ran down her cheeks.

"Give me that watering-can, Amelia
Jane," said the clockwork clown sternly.
When he spoke like that, he had to be
obeyed, so Amelia meekly gave him
the can. But she soon began to look

around for some more water to play with.

This time she found a very naughty thing to do. She found that if she stood on a chair by the wash-basin and turned on the tap, she could make the water spurt out all over the room by putting her hand under the tap. And she waited till the curly-haired doll came by, and then spurted the water all over her!

The curly-haired doll was angry, because the water went on her hair and took out the curl. So she was a straight-haired doll then, and every one thought she looked most peculiar.

"I shall have to put my hair in curl-papers to-night, and they are *so* uncomfortable," sighed the doll. "Oh, how I wish I could *smack* Amelia Jane!"

Well, the clown climbed up to the basin, and with his strong hands he turned off the two taps so very tightly that not even Amelia Jane could turn them on again. So she couldn't play *that* trick any more.

"Never mind!" thought Amelia. "I shall think of something else! What fun it is to play with water!"

Well, she just couldn't get any water from the taps, and the toys felt safe. But Amelia Jane knew somewhere else to get

water. Yes—the goldfish bowl was full of water for the two goldfish to swim in!

The goldfish lived on a table by the wall. Amelia Jane climbed up to the wash-basin and took the sponge from there. It was quite dry. Then she climbed up to the goldfish bowl and looked into the water.

"Can I borrow some of your water?" she asked the fish. And then, without waiting for an answer, she dipped the sponge into the water and made it dripping wet.

Amelia sat on the table and peeped over the edge, waiting for some one to come by. The rabbit and the dog were having a little walk together and were coming near. Amelia Jane giggled.

She waited until they were just underneath, and then she squeezed the sponge gently.

"Drip-drip-drip, drop-drop-drop!" Large cold drops of water fell on to the dog and the rabbit. They were most surprised. They looked up—but Amelia was no longer peeping over the edge of

the table, and they could see nothing. They couldn't understand it.

"I'm wet," said the rabbit, shaking himself.

"And I'm wet too," said the dog, licking himself. "Where did it come from?"

"Can't imagine," said the rabbit. "Perhaps we are mistaken. Come, let us go on with our ramble."

So on they went again, and Amelia Jane watched for them to come back near the table once more. Just as they passed, she held out her sponge and squeezed it hard again.

"Drip-drip-drip, drop-drop-drop!" Down came the water and soaked the dog and the rabbit. How angry they were!

"My ears are dripping," said the rabbit.

"My whiskers are soaked," said the dog. "Let us tell the clown."

Well, as soon as they complained to the clown, he knew quite well it must be Amelia Jane up to her water-tricks again, and he called to her very sternly:

"Amelia Jane! Will you stop soaking every one? It isn't funny, it is very silly, for you will give every one a dreadful cold. Where are you?"

But Amelia Jane wouldn't answer, though she was aching with trying to stop laughing. The clown was angry, and set out to look for her. He came too near the table and Amelia Jane saw him.

"I can't help it!" she said to herself.

"I must throw this nice wet sponge at him!"

So she threw the sponge at the clown, and it hit him full in the middle. He fell down with a thud, and the sponge dripped wet on him from top to toe. He got up and stared angrily round. But he could *not* see Amelia Jane. She was crouching down on the top of the table again, behind the goldfish bowl.

The clown went to talk to the doll, whose hair was now in curl-papers. The rabbit, the dog, the golliwog, and the clockwork mouse came too.

"It's time we stopped Amelia Jane," said the clown. "What about doing something to *her* with water? That would really be a good punishment!"

"But how can we?" asked the doll

with curl-papers. "If we throw the sponge at her, she'll only throw it back. And you've hidden the can so that she can't get it."

Everybody thought hard. And then the clockwork mouse had an idea! He was only a small toy, but he sometimes had surprisingly big ideas.

"I know!" he said. "What about a syphon of soda-water?"

All the toys stared at him as if he were quite mad. "*You* know!" said the mouse. "The thing that the big people keep in the dining-room, and squirt into a glass when they want a drink. I've seen them. What about getting one of those out of the kitchen where they are stored, and having a squirt at Amelia Jane? If she's so fond of water, she might like a bit of squirting!"

The toys laughed. The clockwork clown and the rabbit went out of the nursery and down the passage to the kitchen to see if they could find a syphon. They found one quite easily in the larder. It was terribly heavy. They had to fetch the dog to help them to carry it back to the nursery.

Amelia Jane had got down from the table and was busy tying a new hair-ribbon on her black curls. She was surprised to hear the heavy bumping as the toys carried the syphon in at the door. She turned round and laughed.

"Whatever have you brought that great ugly thing for?" she asked.

"Do you want to know?" said the clown, bringing it right up to her. Before she could answer, the toys pressed on the handle of the syphon, and the soda water squirted out with a tremendous hissing noise, right into Amelia Jane's surprised face!

Good gracious! She was so startled that she fell over! The toys squealed with delight and squirted her on the ground. She got up and ran away in a dreadful fright. But the toys followed her, and squirted her all the way! Oh dear, oh dear! Poor Amelia, what a shock she got! The syphon made such a noise, and the water soaked her and ran down her neck and quite took her breath away!

"Do you like water so much now?" cried the clown. "Do you think it is nice to be soaked? Squirt-squirt-squirt! How do you like to be watered, Amelia Jane?"

Well, Amelia certainly did *not* like it! She squealed and screamed and made such a noise that the toys were really afraid she would wake up every one who was asleep. So they stopped squirting her and quietly took the syphon back to the kitchen.

Poor Amelia Jane! She had to take off all her clothes, even her vest, and dry them by the fire. Even her body was wet, and she had to dry that too, turning herself round and round all night long! I don't think she will play with water again, somehow!

And nobody in the house could *think* where all the soda-water out of that syphon had gone to. Amelia Jane isn't likely to tell them, anyhow!

CHAPTER XI
AMELIA JANE
AND THE MATCHES

THIS is the tale of Amelia Jane and the matches.

Now all boys and girls, unless they are quite old, are warned by their fathers and mothers never to play with matches. And with toys it is just the same. They must never play with matches, in case they get on fire and burn themselves.

But you can guess that Amelia Jane didn't care about any danger! No! If she could get hold of matches you may be sure she would!

There were never any matches left in the nursery, till one day when Jane lighted the fire and forgot to put the

matches back in her
apron pocket, as she
usually did.

Jane left the
box of matches on
the mantelpiece and
Amelia Jane saw it
first, of course
because she was
quite the tallest toy
in the nursery.

"Oooh!" she said,
pointing upwards.
"Matches! If only I
could get them!"

167

"Don't be naughty," said the clock-work clown at once. "You know that children and toys must never touch matches."

"Pooh!" said Amelia Jane rudely.

"Don't pooh at me like that!" said the clockwork clown. "It's rude."

"Pooh, pooh, pooh!" said Amelia Jane. So you can guess she was in one of her naughty moods again.

She stood and thought for a minute. Then she remembered how the cowboy doll had taught her to throw a lasso round anything and jerk it near. If only she could make a loop of rope and throw it carefully, she could get those matches down easily.

She ran to the string-box and opened it. The teddy bear saw her. "If you're thinking of lassoing those matches and getting them down, just let me remind you what happened last time you tried your hand at that!" he said. "You lassoed the bowl of tadpoles, and got them all down your neck."

Amelia Jane took no notice. She got out a long piece of string and made a loop-knot at the end. Then she stood beneath the mantelpiece and threw the string neatly upwards, holding one end in her hand.

"Ooooh!" said all the toys in surprise, because, will you believe it, Amelia Jane got the loop right round the box, and it fell almost at her feet when she pulled the string!

"Aren't I clever!" said Amelia proudly.

"No, you're not, you're just lucky,"
said the clockwork clown. "You're not
to touch those matches, Amelia Jane."

"Pooh!" said Amelia, and she opened
the box. "Now, who wants to see me
strike a match?"

The toys felt frightened. They knew
quite well that matches can set fire to

things and burn them. They ran to the toy cupboard and crept inside, all except the clockwork mouse, and he did badly want to see a match struck.

"I'd like to see some matches struck, please, Amelia," he said, and he ran nearer.

"Well, you shall see a whole lot struck!" said the big doll. "The others have all run away, the sillies. You and I will enjoy ourselves!"

Amelia opened the box. She took out a match. She struck it hard on the side of the

box. "Fizzz-zzz-zzz!" The match lighted and Amelia Jane held it up in the air, watching the bright flame.

The clockwork mouse liked it very much indeed. He thought it was most exciting.

"Please, please, let me light one too," he begged.

"Amelia Jane, if you let the mouse strike a match we'll all come out of the cupboard and smack you," shouted the clockwork clown. "He's too little to do dangerous things like that."

"All right, all right!" said Amelia, striking another match. "I shan't let him. Besides, I want to strike them all myself!"

But before Amelia Jane could strike any more matches there came the sound of steps on the landing outside. The toys flopped down. Amelia ran to the cupboard, throwing the box of matches into a corner. The clockwork mouse ran into the brick-box. So when Jane looked into the nursery, there was no one to be seen at all. Everything was quiet. She had come to put some fresh flowers on the table. Then she dusted round a bit and went downstairs again.

The toys didn't come out for a long time—not until it was night, for they were afraid of being caught. The first toy that came alive was the clockwork mouse. He saw the box

of matches in the corner and was pleased. He ran to them and pushed them along with his nose till he came to a slipper. He popped them into the slipper.

"Aha!" he thought. "Now no one will know where they are, and I can strike as many as I like when the others are not looking!"

Now when all the toys came out of the cupboard they looked very stern indeed. They were angry with Amelia Jane. She had no right to teach the clockwork mouse to play with matches!

The toys sat round Amelia in a circle, and scolded her.

"We shall none of us talk to you for a week," said the teddy bear.

"We shall not play with you at all," said the clockwork clown.

"You will not have any of the sweets out of the toy sweet-shop," said the curly-haired doll.

"And we have hidden your fine new bonnet so that you can't wear it when you go out," said the pink rabbit.

"Pooh!" said Amelia Jane—but not in a very poohy voice. She was upset. She hated not being talked to or played with. It would be horrid not to have any sweets. And oh, fancy hiding her lovely new bonnet so that she couldn't wear it! Amelia Jane felt like crying. She walked over to the window-seat and sat there, sniffing hard. She was very unhappy.

Suddenly the toys heard a curious noise.

"Fizz-zz-zz-zz!"

It was the clockwork mouse striking a match all by himself. The toys stared at him in horror. He struck another and squeaked in delight.

But oh, my goodness me, what do you think happened? His whiskers caught alight! Yes, they really did, and the poor little mouse found himself on fire, with flames burning each side of his little face!

"Sizzle-sizzle!" went his fine whiskers. The mouse squealed in fright and flung away the lighted match. Oh dear—it fell on to an open book and the pages caught alight! The book flamed up, and set light to the brick-box nearby.

"Crackle-crackle!" went the flames merrily. "Crackle-crackle! We're going to eat the book! We're going to eat the brick-box! Then we'll eat the carpet—and the chairs—and the toy cupboard—and all the toys—and the whole house! Crackle, crackle, crackle!"

It was dreadful. The toys stared in horror and couldn't move even a paw, they were so frightened. No wonder they had been warned against playing with matches. This was what happened when they disobeyed!

"Eee-eee-eee!" squealed the poor little clockwork mouse, his whiskers

burning all away. He ran to and fro in pain and fright. All the toys watched and trembled dreadfully.

And what about that big, naughty doll, Amelia Jane! Yes—she was watching too, her face pale with fright. Poor, poor little mouse—how she wished she hadn't shown him how to strike matches! And oh, that book—and the lovely brick-box! Whatever would happen to them all?

"Well, I began it, so I must try and stop it!" cried Amelia Jane. "I remember hearing some one say that if any one got on fire they should be rolled round tightly in a rug to put the flames out. Where, oh, where is a rug?"

"In the dolls' pram!" yelled the teddy bear, who was still too frightened to move.

Amelia Jane ran to the dolls' pram. She snatched up the thick blue rug there and rushed to the little clockwork mouse. She threw the rug all round his little grey body and rolled him up tightly in it, head, tail, and all! She felt the flames trying to burn her hands, and they hurt her, but she didn't stop. She meant to save the little mouse!

The thick rug squashed all the flames out. They died away. There were none left. The clockwork mouse wasn't on fire any more.

But the book and the brick-box were still burning away. Amelia Jane left the mouse and ran to the basin with a jug. She stood on a chair, turned on the tap and filled the jug. Down she climbed and rushed to the brick-box. She threw the water over the flames.

"Sizzle-sizzle!" they said, and died out. They could not go on burning when water was thrown over them. Then Amelia fetched another jug of water and threw it over the burning book.

"Sizzle-sizzle!" said the flames again, and went out. The fire was gone!

The toys came round, looking quite pale. Amelia Jane sat down and began to cry.

"I wish I hadn't touched the matches,

I wish I hadn't!" she sobbed.

"I've got no whiskers now!" wept the poor little clockwork mouse. Sure enough, he hadn't—and he did look funny without them. What a noise Amelia Jane and the mouse made, sobbing together!

"You'll never speak to me or play

with me again," wept Amelia, looking round at the toys. "I might as well go away from here and never come back."

"Now listen, Amelia Jane," said the teddy bear, putting his arm round her. "You did a very wrong thing, and it has caused a lot of damage—but you have done your best to put it right, and you were brave when all of us were too afraid to do anything."

"So we will have to forgive you," said the clown. "We were angry with you when you were bad, but we think you are brave too, so cheer up."

"What about the mouse's whiskers, though—and the burnt book and brick-box?" wept Amelia.

"The mouse will have to do without his whiskers," said the golliwog. "The book was very old and torn, so perhaps it won't matter being burnt; and as for the brick-box, it's only the lid that has been burnt, and I can make a new one with the carpenter's set in the toy cupboard. But look at your own hands—and the front of your dress! They are burnt too!"

"It serves me right," said Amelia Jane. "I'll put some good ointment on my hands, and I'll have to go about with a burnt bit of dress in front. Oh, I'm so glad you've forgiven me, Toys! I won't be naughty again."

Well, the toys didn't believe *that*, of course—they knew Amelia Jane too well! But they were soon good friends again, and, secretly, they couldn't help admiring Amelia Jane for putting out the fire so quickly, and saving the little mouse.

"She's like the little girl in the nursery rhyme," said the bear to the clown. "*You* know—when she's good she's *very*, *very* good—but when she's bad she's horrid!"